SO-DZE-991

Beach Time for Clarence

Written by Michèle Dufresne

Illustrated by Max Stasiuk

PIONEER VALLEY EDUCATIONAL PRESS, INC.

Look at this.

This is my bathing suit.

Look at this.
This is my towel.

Look at this.
This is my hat.

Look at this.
This is my chair.

Look at this.
This is my bucket.

Look at this.
This is my shovel.

Look at this.
This is my tube.

Look at this.
I can swim!